DISNEP

# Star Darlings

# A WISHER'S GUIDE TO STARLAND

DISNEP PRESS

Los Angeles • New York

This book owes its glow and magic to the hard work of the following Wishlings:

Bill Scollon, Caroline LaVelle Egan, Margie Peng, Erin Zimring, Jean-Paul Orpiñas, Scott Piehl, Jeffrey Thomas, John T. Quinn, Wendy Lefkon, Laureen Gleason, Karen Chau, Chris Painter, Carlotta Quattrocolo, Sophia Lin, and Kevin Ramirez.

And a star shout-out to:

Luigi Aimé, Luke Belderes, Isaac Choi, Maurizio De Bellis, Iboix Estudi, Francesco Legramandi, Pernille Ørum-Nielsen, Arianna Rea, Diogo Saito, and Evgeny (Otto) Schmidt.

Printed in the United States of America
First Edition, January 2016
1 3 5 7 9 10 8 6 4 2
F322-8368-0-15324
Library of Congress Control Number: 2015935150
ISBN 978-1-4847-1799-8
Visit www.disneybooks.com

**Disney**

# STARDARLINGS

# A WISHER'S GUIDE TO STARLAND

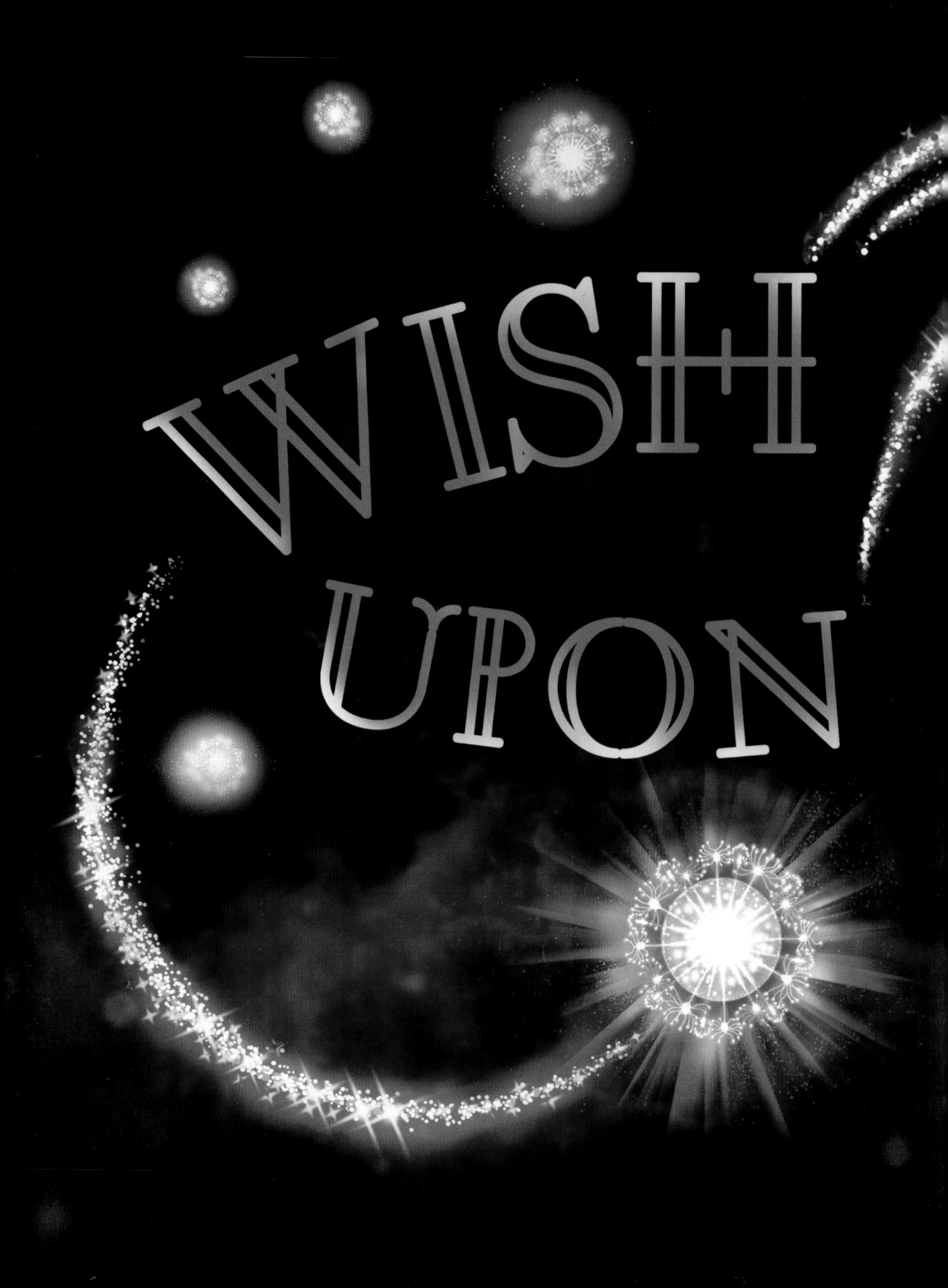
WISH
UPON

YOUR STAR!

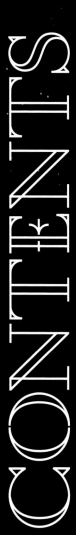

# CONTENTS

The night sky, glittering with billions of stars, reminds us that the universe is full of mystery, magic, and wonder. It inspires our hopes and dreams. Ever since the first girl on Earth looked up at that incredible sky, we've been putting our hopes and dreams into wishes.

But what happens to a wish once we send it out into the universe? Where does it go? Up in the twinkling galaxy, one star stands out from the rest, brighter, fuller, and more **SPARKLY** than the others. But this star is unlike any other star in the sky because it's actually a beautiful, shining world called Starland. And it's where our wishes are collected and cared for until it's time for them to come true.

The fantastical world of Starland is a lot like our own planet. It has oceans, continents, cities, and different seasons. But on Starland, everything glows with positive energy: plants, animals, buildings, and even Starlings, the people who live there. The Starlings' natural glow gets brighter and more beautiful as they age. Then, when their Cycle of Life is complete, Starlings become pure light and join the constellation of ancestors above their world.

Wishes from Earth (known as Wishworld to Starlings) are the key to Starland's existence. The planet relies on the seemingly endless supply of positive wish energy that's released when a wish is granted.

Without it, Starland would go dark forever.

STAR DARLINGS

# 1

## STAR DARLINGS

Young Starlings who have the most potential to be stellar Wish-Granters are chosen to go to wish-granting school, and the most prestigious of these is called Starling Academy. There, girls learn how to make wishes come true and collect the positive wish energy that powers Starland and is essential to their peaceful way of life.

But Starland's energy levels are shrinking. Luckily, Lady Stella, the headmistress of Starling Academy, discovered the oracle of the twelve Star-Charmed Starlings. It inspired her to select twelve Star-Charmed Starling girls to help her with a super-secret plan to save their world.

Coming from different places and walks of life, they will go on dazzling adventures, face tough challenges, and become the most brilliant of friends. These twelve amazing girls are the Star Darlings!

# SAGE

Sage has wanted to be a Wish-Granter ever since she saw her first shooting star. Being admitted to Starling Academy was like a dream come true.

When it comes to energy manipulation, she can out-glow anyone. It's always come easy for her. Even as a baby, Sage could levitate her toys! But because of her natural talents, she sometimes forgets that she has a lot to learn from school.

Sage is a bold, positive force, full of charisma, who always looks on the bright side. She's lighthearted and luminous and finds it easy to make new friends. Sage's confident vibe attracts others into her orbit. But Sage is not all twinkles and starlight. She sometimes says things without thinking and then falls all over herself apologizing!

Sage's mom is a top wish energy scientist and her dad works in the government. She and her twin brothers—who love nothing more than annoying their big sister—grew up in a big rambling house in Starland City.

**YEAR IN STARLING ACADEMY:** First
**HOMETOWN:** Starland City
**BRIGHT DAY:** December 1
**FAVORITE COLOR:** Lavender
**HOBBY:** Playing lead guitar like a rock star.

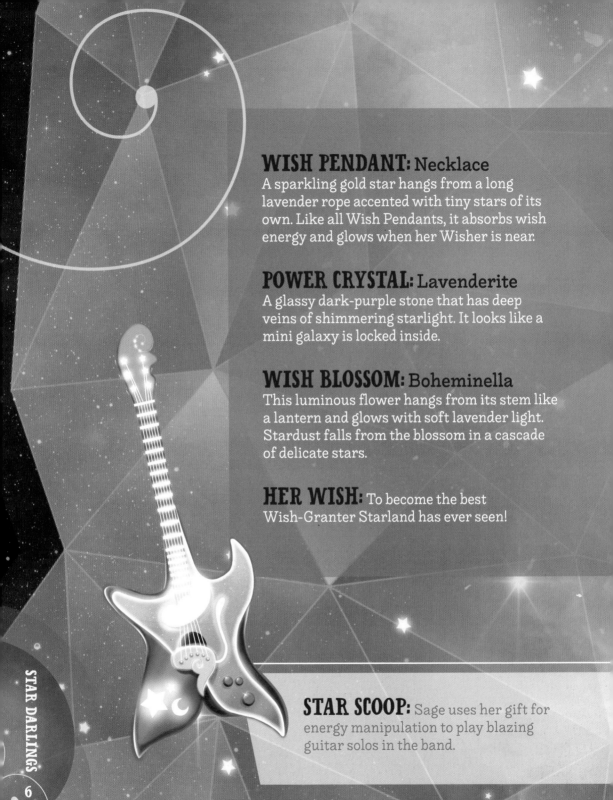

**WISH PENDANT:** Necklace

A sparkling gold star hangs from a long lavender rope accented with tiny stars of its own. Like all Wish Pendants, it absorbs wish energy and glows when her Wisher is near.

**POWER CRYSTAL:** Lavenderite

A glassy dark-purple stone that has deep veins of shimmering starlight. It looks like a mini galaxy is locked inside.

**WISH BLOSSOM:** Boheminella

This luminous flower hangs from its stem like a lantern and glows with soft lavender light. Stardust falls from the blossom in a cascade of delicate stars.

**HER WISH:** To become the best Wish-Granter Starland has ever seen!

**STAR SCOOP:** Sage uses her gift for energy manipulation to play blazing guitar solos in the band.

NECKLACE

LAVENDERITE

BOHEMINELLA

# LIBBY

Libby's parents have absolutely astronomical careers and tons of money. As an only child, Libby grew up never wanting for anything. And the kids in her Radiant Hills neighborhood were just as lucky. Libby thought life was that easy for everyone until a few years ago when she met a girl who'd never had her own doll. Libby gave her one, and the girl's radiant joy and gratitude ignited a spirit of giving in Libby.

Her parents were happy about their daughter's spark of generosity—until she started giving almost all her possessions away! Libby can be a bit impulsive and irresponsible sometimes, but her heart is in the right place.

Now that Libby is at Starling Academy, her parents have stopped giving her spending money. But that's fine with Libby. Helping others is what really stokes her glow. In fact, she stardreams about becoming the student body president so she can help everybody!

**YEAR IN STARLING ACADEMY:** First
**HOMETOWN:** Starland City
**BRIGHT DAY:** October 12
**FAVORITE COLOR:** Pink
**HOBBY:** Playing her top-of-the-line keytar. Finally, the years of piano lessons make sense!

## WISH PENDANT: Necklace

A constellation of golden stars rings Libby's dazzling necklace. Wish energy ripples across the stars. On Wishworld, the necklace will glow to alert Libby when she's close to the right Wisher.

## POWER CRYSTAL: Charmelite

An angular, multifaceted electric-pink jewel that pulses with an inner light. It looks as rugged as any Power Crystal, but this stone is light as air and a bit fragile.

## WISH BLOSSOM: Blushbelle

This bright pink-on-pink flower with curlicue filaments is lovely and delicate. The blossom puffs out a soft kiss of stardust whenever a Starling comes near.

## HER WISH: To give everyone what they need—both on Starland and through wish granting on Wishworld.

**STAR SCOOP:** Libby's mom and dad went supernova furious over Libby's habit of giving practically all her stuff away!

NECKLACE

CHARMELITE

BLUSHBELLE

# LEONA

Leona has all the sparkle it takes to become a top Wish-Granter. But ever since her first glow, all she's really wanted to be is a glittering pop star!

Going to Starling Academy is Leona's way of breaking away from her routine existence in the lifeless town of Flairfield. Her family thinks it's great that Leona has ambition, but they don't get the whole "I have to be in the spotlight" thing. Instead, Leona's parents want her to work as a bookkeeper in her dad's shoe repair shop. But Leona has her head in the stars, and there's no way she's going to let that happen.

Leona doesn't just stand out in a crowd—her super radiance can consume the crowd! But for all her glimmering self-confidence, Leona sometimes forgets that it isn't always about *her* all the time. Even though she loves being the center of attention, she has to remember she's part of a team and get her star charts back in order!

**YEAR IN STARLING ACADEMY:** Third
**HOMETOWN:** Flairfield
**BRIGHT DAY:** August 16
**FAVORITE COLOR:** Gold
**HOBBY:** Singing and performing. What else?

**WISH PENDANT:** Cuff

Leona wears a gold cuff with a bold metallic gold star that sizzles with wish energy. On Wishworld, the bracelet helps Leona find her Wisher.

**POWER CRYSTAL:** Glisten paw

These rough-cut yellow-gold jewels cast a startlingly bright golden light.

**WISH BLOSSOM:** Golden roar

This bright, shiny gold flower cannot be overlooked. Its intense light pours out like a spotlight. Symmetrical layers of pointy petals set off the perfect golden star in the center.

**HER WISH:** To be the most famous pop star on Starland!

**STAR SCOOP:** Leona can't stand being cold. She loves lying out in the sun in the Time of Lumiere.

CUFF

GLISTEN PAW

GOLDEN ROAR

# VEGA

Vega works as hard as any student at Starling Academy— and probably harder than she needs to. But that kind of laser focus is what you need if you want to be the brightest star in school.

Vega grew up with her mom in a small apartment in the center of a dull factory town, and she realized that her ticket to a different kind of life was focusing on school and aiming for the stars; after that, it was pretty much all straight As.

Yep, Vega is something of a perfectionist.

Vega makes lists and checks them twice, sometimes even three times. She's a planner, and it's helped her so far. But when it comes to wish granting, she has to learn to use her instincts and intuition. Even Lady Stella told her she needs to relax a bit and take time out for a glimmer of fun. Vega loves to dance, and playing the bass guitar in the Star Darlings' band really makes her sparkle!

**YEAR IN STARLING ACADEMY:** Second
**HOMETOWN:** Kaleidoscope City
**BRIGHT DAY:** September 1
**FAVORITE COLOR:** Blue
**HOBBY:** Playing bass guitar with
     ultra precision.

## WISH PENDANT: Belt

Vega's belt buckle is a perfectly shaped star with a wide border. On Starland, its glow reminds Vega to always do her best. When she's on a Wish Mission, the glow helps her pinpoint her Wisher.

## POWER CRYSTAL: Queezle

Sparkling crystalline blue nuggets are held together by their own internal magnetic force. Their seemingly chaotic arrangement actually represents a precise mathematical equation.

## WISH BLOSSOM: Bluebubble

Deep blue gives way to icy blue in the petals of this compact illuminated flower. Glowing points of light orbit the blossom. Its petals open and close with such regularity that you can use it to tell time.

## HER WISH: To be the top student at Starling Academy.

## STAR SCOOP: Vega loves crunching through fallen leaves on a chilly day in the Time of Letting Go.

BELT

QUEEZLE

BLUEBUBBLE

# SCARLET

Scarlet went from being homeschooled while on tour with her parents to being with girls her own age all day, every day. It hasn't been easy. To her classmates, Scarlet seems to be in a completely different orbit. And that's just fine with her. She's confident, strong, and independent.

Scarlet's parents are super-stellar classical musicians who, for as long as Scarlet can remember, have played in the planet's most star-studded concert halls. As an only child on the road with her family most of the year, Scarlet had to learn how to entertain herself. Scarlet knows she needs to work on opening up to the other girls, but she's been a loner her whole life. She's just not a warm, fuzzy, touchy-feely kind of girl.

Scarlet's wish-granting potential is off the charts. Now if she could only grant her own wish—to find a place where she feels comfortable letting her inner light shine through.

**YEAR IN STARLING ACADEMY:** Third
**HOMETOWN:** New Prism
**BRIGHT DAY:** November 3
**FAVORITE COLOR:** Black
**HOBBY:** Skateboarding and attacking the drums.

**WISH PENDANT:** Boots
Rows of star-shaped buckles on Scarlet's boots do
more than secure them to her feet. They also alert
her that she's close to her Wisher!

**POWER CRYSTAL:** Ravenstone
A complex jumble of dark red-black crystals that
glows with a restless burgundy light. The random
pattern of gems sits atop an unstable, pliable
center.

**WISH BLOSSOM:** Punkypow
Sturdy burgundy leaves cup a burst of creamy
star-shaped petals. The blossom's light
mysteriously dims and brightens for no apparent
reason. The flower smells a bit like licorice.

**HER WISH:** To live on Wishworld!

**STAR SCOOP:** Scarlet's parents were
thrilled when she showed an interest in
music. But they wanted her to take up the
starflooty, a delicate woodwind instrument.
Instead, Scarlet's rebellious nature led her to
the drums!

BOOTS

RAVENSTONE

PUNKYPOW

# CASSIE

Cassie's star journey has been a bumpy one to say the least. After losing her parents at an early age, Cassie was raised by her uncle. He had to travel a lot for business and often left Cassie to fend for herself. She found comfort in charting constellations and reading books. To this day, she reads constantly.

Cassie is supersmart, loyal, and a logical thinker. She's really happy to be at Starling Academy, and more than anything, she wants to have friends, but she's shy and tends to hold back her true feelings. The truth is she misses her parents a lot. Cassie appears to be guarded and closed off, but what she's really afraid of is that if she gets close to someone, they'll leave her like her parents did.

Cassie's best friend is a glowfur named Bitty. Bitty was Cassie's mom's pet glowfur years and years ago. It's true that the academy doesn't allow students to keep pets in the dorm, but Cassie marches to the signal of her own pulsar.

**YEAR IN STARLING ACADEMY:** First
**HOMETOWN:** Old Prism
**BRIGHT DAY:** July 6
**FAVORITE COLOR:** White
**HOBBY:** Curling up with a really good mystery book.

**WISH PENDANT:** Star glasses

With rims lit by wish energy, Cassie's glasses are perfect for reading late at night without disturbing her roommate. On Wish Missions, the glowing frames signal the presence of her Wisher.

**POWER CRYSTAL:** Lunalite

A pinkish-white moonlight hangs like a mist around these faceted oblong jewels.

**WISH BLOSSOM:** Silverbella

This moon-shaped flower is packed with tiny pink-and-white petals that radiate from the plant's center. A gentle pale glow sparkles with strawberry-scented flecks of starlight.

**HER WISH:** To be more independent and confident and less fearful.

**STAR SCOOP:** Cassie is more comfortable sharing her feelings in a note than saying them out loud.

STAR GLASSES

LUNALITE

SILVERBELLA

# PIPER

Piper seems to float through life as if she's on her own astral plane. She's ethereal and speaks with a voice that's calming and smooth as silk. But sometimes she gives the other girls the heebie-jeebies. She's psychic and is always telling her friends about visions she's had and looking for spirits.

To Piper's credit, her upbringing was unusual. She lived in a mysterious old house far out in the countryside with her energetic grandmother and an aloof older brother. The house had a reputation for being haunted, and practically no one ever came to visit. But that was fine with Piper. She made friends with the luminous spirits and chatted with them every day!

When Piper doesn't have her head in the cosmos, she's pretty fun. She's also super artistic and writes beautiful poetry. And her connection to the magic all around her makes her a perfect Star Darling.

**YEAR IN STARLING ACADEMY:** Second
**HOMETOWN:** The Gloom Flats
**BRIGHT DAY:** March 4
**FAVORITE COLOR:** Seafoam green
**HOBBY:** Daydreaming and writing poems.

## WISH PENDANT: Bracelets

Three sea-green bracelets decorate Piper's wrist. A circle of star-shaped jewels is embedded in each bangle. They radiate golden wish energy. On Wishworld, the stars help her find her way to her assigned Wisher.

## POWER CRYSTAL: Dreamalite

This misty aqua gem is ringed by sparkling stardust that revolves around it like a solar system of tiny moons.

## WISH BLOSSOM: Sleepibelle

The blue-green blossom hangs down from its stem and flares out like a full silky skirt. Light trims a double set of ruffles along the bottom edges. The flower slowly swishes back and forth to a rhythm all its own. It has a fragrance of honey and vanilla.

## HER WISH: To become the best version of herself she can possibly be, and to share that by writing books.

**STAR SCOOP:** Piper is working on an epic poem about wishes. She expects it to be four hundred thousand lines long. But she's only on line thirty!

BRACELETS

DREAMALITE

SLEEPIBELLE

# ASTRA

Astra reaches for the stars in everything she does. She's strong and unstoppable. Growing up, she earned a galaxy of star trophies for athletics. She's mastered practically every sport, from energy volley to star bases to star ball. In fact, it was Starling Academy's star ball team that made Astra want to apply to the school in the first place. Now she's the team's most stellar player.

But coming to Starling Academy, where everyone wants to be the best, presented Astra with new challenges. She learned that she had to bring a sizzling new level of energy to her athletics *and* her studies if she was going to stay on top.

All this focus on winning has its downside. Astra can be brash and act like she's the center of the universe, and that can push friends out of her orbit.

**YEAR IN STARLING ACADEMY:** Second
**HOMETOWN:** Gleemington
**BRIGHT DAY:** April 9
**FAVORITE COLOR:** Red
**HOBBY:** Competing in sports or
just about anything!

## WISH PENDANT: Wristband

One large star, set in a pulsing ring of golden wish energy, adorns Astra's practical wristband. On Wishworld, the glowing wristband helps Astra confirm that she has found her Wisher.

## POWER CRYSTAL: Quarrelite

This asteroid-shaped deep-red jewel has an outer layer of interlinked ribs that appear to be holding the crystal together.

## WISH BLOSSOM: Florafierce

What this strong, bold flower lacks in subtlety it makes up for in raw beauty. Fiery-red petals ring a center mound of small, tightly packed leaves. Glowing stardust rises from the middle of the blossom as if in a never-ending victory celebration.

## HER WISH: To be the most famous athlete on Starland! And to win … at everything!

## STAR SCOOP: Astra loves to play sports in the pouring rain!

WRISTBAND

QUARRELITE

FLORAFIERCE

# TESSA

From the time she began to sparkle, Tessa showed a love of the pleasures in life, like soft, luxurious blankets, long naps, and gourmet meals. Lucky for Tessa, her mom is a renowned Starland chef who taught Tessa how to create delicious meals from the fresh and abundant herbs and produce that grew on their family's farm.

Tessa may enjoy creature comforts, but she will still put all her effort into any project she decides to tackle. Her approach to life is "Work hard, play hard!"

Tessa's friends and her sister, Gemma, will tell you she's also super loyal to those she loves—and that includes animals as well as people. She has a deep connection with Starland's magical creatures. Just be careful when trying to win an argument with Tessa. She's always convinced she's right, and she can be incredibly stubborn!

**YEAR IN STARLING ACADEMY:** Third
**HOMETOWN:** Solar Springs
**BRIGHT DAY:** May 18
**FAVORITE COLOR:** Emerald green
**HOBBY:** Cooking for her friends
and trying new foods.

## WISH PENDANT: Brooch

This large multidimensional silvery star set on a circular backing softly pulses with pale green light. On Wishworld, the brooch works like a compass to lead Tessa to her Wisher.

## POWER CRYSTAL: Gossamer

Tiny gold stars orbit this surfboard-shaped rich-green jewel. It's delicate and translucent in appearance, but don't let that fool you. It's just as potent as any other Power Crystal.

## WISH BLOSSOM: Vertessema

Shaped like an amusement park ride, this festive flower features spokes of green filament holding a wheel of golden stars. The slightest breeze makes the spokes ripple in perfect sync, like well-choreographed star dancers. The center of the flower emits a soft whistling sound.

## HER WISH: To be successful enough to enjoy a life of luxury.

**STAR SCOOP:** Tessa's favorite season is the Time of New Beginnings. She loves rolling down a hill of freshly mowed grass!

BROOCH.

GOSSAMER

VERTESSEMA

# ADORA

No detail is too small for Adora. She loves analyzing just about anything! She's cool and clearheaded; Adora's opinion is that emotion just gets in the way of good decision making.

While Adora spends her days in the lab, she also loves to put on a glittering dress and go out dancing, too! When she got her first microscope, the very first thing she looked at was a sequin. From that moment on, Adora has been dedicated to the science of fashion and style. Whether she's trying to create a new sparkly fabric or stardust eyeliner, Adora throws herself wholeheartedly into her work.

Adora's technical skills are at the genius level, but her personal skills need an upgrade. Some of her friends say that Adora can be cold and detached, as if she's constantly analyzing everything around her—which, actually, she is!

**YEAR IN STARLING ACADEMY:** Third
**HOMETOWN:** Starland City
**BRIGHT DAY:** February 14
**FAVORITE COLOR:** Sky blue
**HOBBY:** Problem solving, especially in math and science!

## WISH PENDANT: Watch

This precision timepiece and computer is framed with a ribbon of ice-blue wish energy. On Wishworld, the five points of the watch work like a compass to point the way to Adora's Wisher.

## POWER CRYSTAL: Azurica

Rectangular blue pillars of different sizes are all gathered under a golden dome. Above, an upside-down dewdrop supports it all.

## WISH BLOSSOM: Skywinkle

This blue flower sparkles as if dusted with diamonds. More subtle than most Wish Blossoms, the skywinkle seems to contain the mysteries of the universe; the more you stare at it, the more layers it reveals.

## HER WISH: To be the top fashion designer on Starland.

**STAR SCOOP:** Adora wants to invent a stretchy fabric that responds to music. If she succeeds, your clothes will literally dance with you!

WATCH

AZURICA

SKYWINKLE

# CLOVER

Clover has had a wildly unusual childhood. She's part of the Flying Molensa Family, one of Starland's most illustrious circus acts! Her extended family is made up of acrobats, jugglers, star swallowers—you name it. As you might imagine, Clover has a lot of unique talents, such as doing backflips, making cotton candy, and playing guitar while standing on a galloping galliope!

Though Clover can play almost any instrument, what she really loves to do is write celestial songs and deejay, so she's a perfect addition to the Star Darlings' band.

Clover is a born performer, always cracking jokes and making people laugh. But sometimes she has a hard time turning off the performer in her. Still, she's always super supportive of her friends and helps keep the vibe light.

**YEAR IN STARLING ACADEMY:** Second
**HOMETOWN:** Everywhere!
**BRIGHT DAY:** January 5
**FAVORITE COLOR:** Purple
**HOBBY:** Being a DJ and writing songs.

## WISH PENDANT: Barrette

Clover's barrette is not only great for keeping her hair in place, but it's great at locating Wishers and can soak up huge amounts of wish energy.

## POWER CRYSTAL: Panthera

This deep-purple jewel reflects magenta and mauve tones as light moves across its facets. A dangling orb serves as a counterpoint to the larger polished angular stone.

## WISH BLOSSOM: Purple piphany

Five rings of pale purple light create virtual petals that orbit the flower's physical structure. An umbrella of plush purple leaves stands atop a multicolored stem. Brushing against the leaves releases the aroma of black pepper and blueberry.

## HER WISH: To be the best songwriter and DJ on Starland.

**STAR SCOOP:** Living on campus is a big adjustment for Clover. She's never stayed in one place for more than a week!

BARRETTE

PANTHERA

PURPLE PIPHANY

# GEMMA

Gemma is popular and hilarious, and she's also super chatty. She pretty much says anything and everything that pops into her head. There's never a moment of silence around Gemma. When she was younger, she even talked to farm animals because they were such great listeners.

Gemma loves her big sister, Tessa, but she wants to get out from under Tessa's glow. Everybody loves Tessa, so Gemma feels she has to be "on" all the time to stand out. She wants everyone to like her, and if she even *thinks* someone doesn't, she stresses about it for days.

Gemma and Tessa are part of a family that likes to tease; it's how they show affection. But Gemma's starcasm can offend others without her meaning it to. Gemma needs to learn how to rein in her energy.

**YEAR IN STARLING ACADEMY:** First
**HOMETOWN:** Solar Springs
**BRIGHT DAY:** June 2
**FAVORITE COLOR:** Orange
**HOBBY:** Cracking up her friends.

**WISH PENDANT:** Earrings
Gemma's big bright earrings make a bold fashion statement. Their glow helps guide Gemma to her Wisher.

**POWER CRYSTAL:** Scatterite
This egg-shaped crystal has a perfectly smooth surface. The stone is a lustrous milky orange sprinkled with stardust.

**WISH BLOSSOM:** Chatterburst
This vibrant bright-orange flower is bursting with energy. Filaments hung with glowing stardust look like a swarm of bobbing fireflies. The flower turns to face whoever is near to capture attention. It smells like orange and vanilla ice pops.

**HER WISH:** To be valued for her opinions on everything.

**STAR SCOOP:** The only time Gemma is quiet is when she's drifting across a peaceful lake in a rowboat.

EARRINGS

SCATTERITE

CHATTERBURST

# THE BAND

Leona had the idea to form a band. When she held tryouts, tons of students came to audition. A lot of them *thought* they were star musicians, but they didn't have the right sparkle. When the results were posted, the girls who made the band were over the moon. Vega was chosen because she's a virtuoso on the deep-bass guitar. Sage was picked as the lead guitarist. Scarlet got in because she proved she was the best drummer by far. And Libby's lifetime of piano lessons made her a perfectly brilliant keytar player. Of course, Leona was the lead singer!

The girls practice as often as they can and love performing together. Their special brand of sparkle rock is earning them a lot of fans!

# BECOMING FRIENDS

Most of the Star Darlings had never even met before Lady Stella brought them all together in her office. From the start, the girls were sure they could work together, but there was no guarantee they'd become friends.

The mix of ages and personalities has made for some unbreakable friendships and others that are a little bit shaky. But one thing is for sure— the Star Darlings are always there for one another when it matters most.

## THE COMPETITIVE ONES:

Leona, Astra, Adora, and Vega like to come out on top. Each wants to be the brightest star at what she does—Leona at performing, Astra at sports, Adora at fashion science, and Vega at . . . well, everything!

## THE INDEPENDENT ONES:

Cassie and Scarlet are more comfortable being by themselves and don't really care much for the group scene. They both would like to be a little more social; it's just hard for them.

## THE FUN ONES:

Sage, Libby, Gemma, and Tessa love to have fun above all else. They appreciate a good joke and can dish out—and take—a certain amount of good-spirited teasing and starcasm.

## THE ARTISTIC ONES:

Clover and Piper are both amazingly creative writers. Clover writes all the songs for the band, and Piper's poetry sparkles. They really understand each other.

# WISH ENERGY

## WISH ENERGY

When a wish is granted, wish energy is released. Starlings are experts at gathering that positive energy and using it to power Starland. But when energy levels began to mysteriously fall, Lady Stella decided it was time to act. She searched through Starland's ancient tomes and found what she thought was the answer.

It's well-known that wishes made by young Wishlings— pure wishes straight from the heart—produce the greatest amount of positive wish energy. An ancient text contained an oracle, a prophecy, about twelve Star-Charmed Starlings. It predicted that if the right twelve Starlings were brought together to grant the wishes of young Wishlings, an astronomical amount of wish energy would be created!

After considering scores of students, Lady Stella believed she'd found the twelve girls who could fulfill the oracle's prophecy. But students aren't supposed to go to Wishworld until they graduate, so Lady Stella's scheme to send the Star Darlings on Wish Missions to Wishworld before graduation depends on total secrecy.

If the daring plan succeeds, the Star Darlings will bring back more positive wish energy than hundreds—maybe thousands—of traditional Wish-Granters ever could. And that just might be enough to solve Starland's energy crisis.

# WISH ORBS

When a Wisher makes a wish, something truly breathtaking happens. The wish takes the form of a tiny iridescent ball of energy called a Wish Orb. The orb, invisible to Wishlings, rises into the night sky and joins thousands of other wishes as they zip through space. Destination: Starland!

★ **BELIEVE IN THE POWER OF A WISH.**

# THE WISH-HOUSE

Cascades of Wish Orbs fall steadily on Starland and are channeled into the magnificent Wish-House. There's nothing quite like it anywhere else in the universe. Golden waterfalls of pure wish energy stream down its sides into rivers of power. The Wish-House is one of the many places from which positive energy flows to cities, towns, and homes all over Starland.

Inside the Wish-House, Wish Orbs will grow quickly and take on the appearance of a fluffy ball. When a good wish is ready to be granted, which can take from a few minutes to a few years, the orb radiates a magical sparkly glow!

Once it begins to sparkle, the orb has a short life cycle. When a Starling goes on a Wish Mission, she has to grant the wish before the orb dies. If she fails, the chance for that Wishling's dream to come true is gone forever.

After a Wish-Granter successfully helps grant a wish, she returns to Starland with the positive wish energy that she has collected in her Wish Pendant. That positive energy is released inside the Wish-House and becomes part of the golden energy flowing out of the Wish-House.

✦ **POSITIVE WISHES MAKE THE WORLD A HAPPIER PLACE.**

# WISH BLOSSOMS

When a Wish-Granter fulfills her first wish, the Wish Orb blossoms into a beautiful luminescent flower. Earning their first Wish Blossom is an honor that all Starlings respect and cherish. And, because no two wishes are exactly the same, every Wish Blossom is unique. These special Wish Blossoms eventually turn silver, and the Silver Blossom is then moved to the Hall of Granted Wishes as a glittering tribute to the power of wishes.

**YOU HAVE THE POWER TO MAKE YOUR DREAMS COME TRUE.**

# STAR DARLINGS' WISH-CAVERN

The Star Darlings' Wish-Cavern was built inside a labyrinth of underground caves, as a place where they could meet privately. It is where they receive their top-secret missions, and where Lady Stella presents the first Wish Blossom earned by each Star Darling once her mission is completed successfully. The Wish Blossoms are not only one of a kind, but also contain something extra-special. When the blossoms open, inside each flower is a Power Crystal. The Star Darlings, as the "star-charmed" chosen ones, are the first and only Wish-Granters to ever receive Power Crystals!

# SD WISH BLOSSOMS

After each Star Darling grants her first wish,
she receives a unique Wish Blossom.

## BOHEMINELLA
Sage's blossom glows
with lavender light.

## PUNKYPOW
This flower is dark and
mysterious, just like its
owner, Scarlet.

## GOLDEN ROAR
Like Leona, this bloom
is bright and shiny.

## BLUSHBELLE
Libby's flower releases
puffs of sparkling stardust.

## BLUEBUBBLE
The petals of Vega's bud are
deep blue and precise.

## CHATTERBURST
Just like Gemma, her flower
is an attention-grabbing beauty.

## SKYWINKLE
The blossom that Adora
earns glitters with stardust.

# POWER CRYSTALS

Inside each Wish Blossom is a special Power Crystal. The crystals have a secret cosmic power that makes them key to the success of Lady Stella's plan!

## LAVENDERITE
A universe of stars sparkles inside Sage's Power Crystal.

## RAVENSTONE
Scarlet's stone is as complex as she is.

## GLISTEN PAW
Leona's crystal shines with a brilliant golden light.

## CHARMELITE
The color of this airy gem is perfect for Libby.

## QUEEZLE

Vega's stone is so dense it has its own gravity field.

## DREAMALITE

Piper's crystal holds a vast hidden power.

## QUARRELITE

Sparks of energy race across Astra's asteroid-shaped stone.

## LUNALITE

Faint pink moonlight glows from Cassie's crystal.

## PANTHERA

Light seems to skip across Clover's faceted stone.

## GOSSAMER

Tessa's delicate crystal is surprisingly powerful.

## SCATTERITE

Gemma's smooth stone holds an intricate inner structure.

## AZURICA

The faceted pillars of Adora's crystal multiply its power.

# BAD AND IMPOSSIBLE WISH ORBS

When a Wishling makes a bad wish, that wish's orb arrives on Starland along with all the others. But once it enters Starland's atmosphere, Wish Gatherers direct the Bad Wish Orb to the Negative Energy Facility.

Impossible Wish Orbs are wishes for things such as world peace, cures for incurable diseases, and the end of world hunger. Impossible Wishes are beyond the power of Starlings to grant, no matter how badly they may want to. Impossible Wish Orbs get to be in the Wish House, but are kept in a separate area in case the Wisher changes the wish to something possible to fulfill.

## BAD WISHES.
I wish my friend would fail.
I wish I could make people do anything I want.
I wish my enemy would get hurt.

## IMPOSSIBLE WISHES.
I wish all diseases would disappear.
I wish people could live forever.
I wish my pillow was a marshmallow.

ENERGY

# NEGATIVE ENERGY FACILITY

As soon as a Bad Wish Orb makes its way onto Starland, it is transported to the Negative Energy Facility, which was built in an isolated area. Starlings don't want to risk any chance of the wish's being granted and releasing its negative wish energy. If those wishes were somehow granted, their combined negative energy could destroy Starland!

Of course, there's always the hope that bad wishes can be turned into good wishes, but that almost never happens. If it does, an incredible amount of positive energy is released.

★ **A BAD WISH IS A WISH WASTED.**

★ **NEGATIVE WISHES HURT THE HEART.**

STARLAND

## STARLAND

The planet of Starland is a bright, lush, and vividly colored world. Wish energy circulates through the air both invisibly and as misty clouds of color. Rivulets of golden energy flow through cities and towns in narrow canals. Every surface on Starland sparkles and glows. All of it is concealed by a powerful radiant halo that, from afar, gives the planet the appearance of a vibrant but typical yellow star.

But this world of superstar technology and unrivaled natural wonders is more fragile than most Starlings realize. Few know it, but Starland is facing its greatest challenge yet.

# HOME, SWEET STAR

Starland is dotted with communities of Starlings, from isolated family farms to the planet's glimmering capital.

## STARLAND CITY

### population five million

The largest city on Starland is also its capital. Starland City is glittering and hectic. Rivers of wish energy power the city. In the center is a government district, packed with official buildings. There are also several important universities, parks, and art galleries. As in all of Starland, a sparkling-clean and free mass-transit system makes getting around as easy as catching a falling star. A popular tourist stop is the neighborhood of Radiant Hills, where star-lebrity sightings are common. But visitors are advised to stay away from Dimtown, the home of many under-glowing Starlings.

# NEW PRISM

## population two million

This port city is an important hub for commercial trade and banking. Starlings can get star-designer samples off the rack for huge discounts in the glossy fashion district. It's an intergalactic shopper's paradise! Where Starland City is more formal and fast-paced, New Prism is casual and easygoing.

# KALEIDOSCOPE CITY

## population three hundred thousand

Kaleidoscope City is a factory town. But on Starland, that doesn't mean it's dirty. With no air or water pollution, Kaleidoscope City's colorful downtown is a bona fide tourist destination. Especially known for things made of metal, the city is proud of its production output and uses the motto: "If it's made right, it's made in KC."

# SOLAR SPRINGS

## population eight hundred

Hilly and rural, Solar Springs has few businesses of its own. Residents of the area have to travel to another town for anything more than basic groceries and hardware. Farms and ranches are set far apart like far-flung stars. It's a lonely place for some, but others thrive on the solitude.

## FLAIRFIELD, population thirty thousand

Flairfield is a pleasant, sleepy little town. A charming downtown area offers practically anything a Starling needs. There is a large gleaming park that's home to the annual town picnic. Some may call Flairfield dull, but communities such as this are the backbone of Starland.

## GLEEMINGTON, population ten thousand

This twinkling small town is a great place to raise a family. Everybody knows and looks out for one another. The local school athletic programs are a source of stratospheric civic pride and the town's primary source of entertainment. There's a small commercial area with a bank, a crystal ice-pop stand, and a general store.

## THE GLOOM FLATS, population few and far between

The name Gloom Flats is a pretty accurate description of this area. It's a vast swath of sparsely populated land that is home to isolated homes and a few run-down farms. A perpetual grayness seems to hang over the place. Few venture through, and fewer still can stand to live there.

## OLD PRISM, population two hundred thousand

Old Prism is known for being an original settlement of Starland. Filled with beautiful buildings that once housed Starland's founding mothers, it's a place with a lot of civic pride and a rich history. It has become a folksy tourist destination by day, but at night it's a sleepy little town.

# THE SHIMMERING SEASONS

The seasons on Starland mirror those on Wishworld. Each one glows with enchantment in its own special way.

## THE TIME OF NEW BEGINNINGS

During this season of renewal, the days get warmer and longer. The air smells fresh and clean, and new plants rise from the rich gold-flecked soil. Shimmering rain nourishes the glowing plants and gives everything an extra sparkle. Everything seems possible at this cheerful time of year.

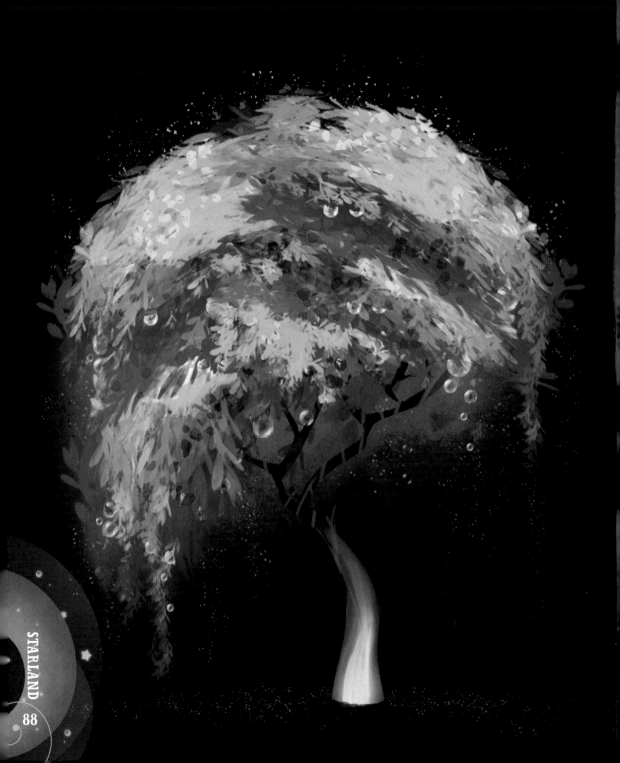

# THE TIME OF LUMIERE

The hottest days of the year are perfect for hiking, swimming, picnicking, and playing games of star ball. Warm crystal-clear nights make this the best season for stargazing, too. Star charts help Starlings locate their ancestors in the brilliant night sky.

# THE TIME OF LETTING GO

Harvest time brings cooler days and the bounty of Starland's crops. Tree leaves turn vibrant colors and fall to the ground. Animals prepare for the cold months ahead. Many Starlings enjoy the simple pleasures of the season, such as jumping into piles of dried leaves or sipping hot cocomoon juice around a campfire.

## THE TIME OF SHADOWS

This is the coldest time of year. The trees are bare, and many animals fall into a deep sleep inside cozy burrows. Starlings have to bundle up to go outside. Icy flecks decorate tree branches with glimmering crystals. As the season gets colder, feathery snowflakes blanket the landscape. Many Starlings brave the cold to go sledding and ice-skating and to make snow-Starlings.

# GROWING AND GLOWING

The world is sprinkled with botanical gardens where Starlings can enjoy the wide variety of radiant flora. One of the nicest is Serenity Gardens. Set on an island in Luminous Lake, the gardens can be seen from Starling Academy. Many of Starland's abundant species of shimmering plants are also edible. How perfect for a world where everyone is vegetarian!

## GLORANGE TREE

This tree is tall, with long branches that radiate out from its center. Late in the Time of Lumiere, the branches are heavy with big orange fruit that has a sweet-and-sour flavor.

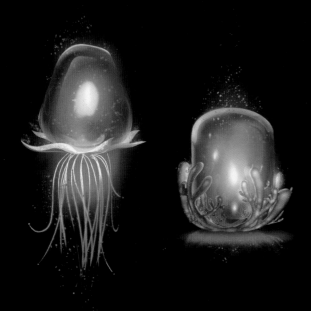

## DRUDERWUMP

This is a barrel-like bush capable of pulling up its own roots and rolling like a tumbleweed, then planting itself again.

## FEATHERJAFFER

The delicate leaves of this glittering perennial taste a little bitter, but they're delicious sautéed or in a salad. Many believe featherjaffer has special healing properties.

## BALLUM BLOSSOM TREE

Pink and white blossoms make this tree especially lovely. At night, the flowers light up with a soft shimmering glow. The fruit of the ballum blossom tree is a sweet red berry. It's eaten raw or baked into pastries.

# COSMIC CREATURES

Starland's glowing animals are friendly, peaceful, and love to have fun. Just like Starlings, the animals of Starland are vegetarians. The positive wish energy that fuels the planet also nourishes the plants the creatures eat. These are a few of the planet's unique species.

## FLUTTERFOCUSES
are brightly colored flying bugs with illuminated wings. They travel in swarms. It's considered good luck to have one land on you and tickle your nose.

## GLOWFURS

come out at night to feed on flowers. They fly on gossamer wings that are barely strong enough to hold up their plump bodies. Cassie has a pet glowfur named Bitty.

## GLIONS

might look ferocious, but they're really sweet and gentle. The animals' multicolored manes shimmer with light. As they walk, they leave paths of star-sparkle footprints behind them.

## MOONBUGS

come out every Star Night, filling the skies with the magical glow from their antennas. These sweet, silly little bugs aren't out to "bug" anyone. They just want to soak up the light of the many moons that fill the solar system and sing their Moonbug tunes.

## GALLIOPES

can be shy and standoffish, but you'll never have a more loyal pet. Starlings ride galliopes, and the animals enjoy racing.

## TWINKELOPES

are majestic herd animals. The male twinkelope has imposing antlers with star-shaped horns, while the female has an iridescent mane and flowing tail. Found in colder climes, they roam the gleaming tundra, feasting on shimmer grass. Their trumpeting call sounds like the lowest note on a hornblatt.

# STARLICIOUS TREATS

Markets on Starland are overflowing with all kinds of brightly colored and delicious fruits, nuts, and veggies. And thanks to wish energy technology, farmers are able to get their produce to stores as soon as it's picked. Farm to table in just hours—talk about fresh! Here's a look at what you might find on a typical menu.

## COCOMOONS

Inside the husk of the large cocomoon bean is a sweet and creamy fruit with an iridescent glow. It tastes especially good on the night following a full moon. Cocomoon juice is one of the most popular drinks on Starland.

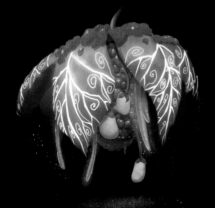

## GARBLE GREENS

Can you imagine mixed vegetables all growing on one plant? Starlings can't get enough of the stuff. Garble greens are served in salads, sautéed, roasted, or made into stew.

## LIGHTTUCE

Leafy lighttuce is crisp and refreshing. It has a mellow green glow that makes it look extra appealing.

## ZOOMBERRY CAKE

This is a traditional Starland food, which happens to go great with a cup of Zing. The cake is made with the pink berries of the zoomberry bush. A party without zoomberry cake is no party at all!

## OZZIEFRUIT

This popular fruit grows on trees and is usually eaten raw or cooked into pies. Ozziefruit orchards are all around Starling Academy.

## ZING

Students love hanging out in a Zing house, chatting with their friends while sipping hot cups of Zing. Brewed from bright tiny leaves, Zing is a favorite on campus—especially if you have to stay up late studying.

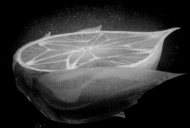

# STAR TECH

Technology on Starland is way more advanced than on Wishworld. That's because of the powerful wish energy that crisscrosses the planet, and it's totally free! The positive energy travels through the air, below the ground, and across the surface of Starland. Wish energy powers every machine, computer, and gadget ever invented by Starlings.

## STAR-ZAP

Starlings rely on their Star-Zaps for nearly everything, from basic holographic communication to scheduling alerts, news, and star charting. And because there's no actual money on Starland, Starlings also use Star-Zaps as their wallets. But the Star Darlings' Star-Zaps have extra specialized features that help guide them through the wish-granting process on Wishworld.

## GLAMERA

This easy-to-use image recorder takes holographic movies and still photos at the touch of a finger. It will then play back the recording in miniature or project it into the room. Startastic!

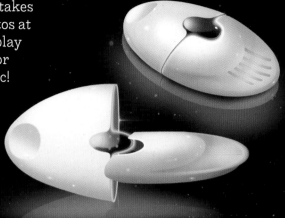

## SPARKLE SHOWERS

Starlings bathe daily in an energy shower to keep their sparkling skin looking and feeling radiant.

## TOOTHLIGHT

Starlings are into staying clean and being healthy. This powerful light tool cleans their teeth so well that there's no need to floss. And, bonus, it gets rid of bad breath, too!

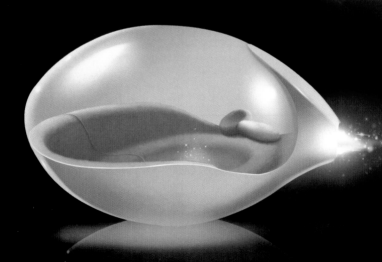

## STARCAR POD

These light, shimmering vehicles are designed for one rider only. They're speedy and nimble but small and have limited entertainment options.

## MULTIRIDER STARCAR

The larger swiftcar can carry up to eight passengers. Voice-controlled, hands-off steering means the whole family can play games, share a meal, or even nap as the swiftcar glides over the highways.

Getting around on Starland is super easy. Wish energy powers all the vehicles, from single-seat scooters to mass-transit trains, so there's no exhaust fumes or pollution. Most vehicles don't even have wheels; they move on a cushion of invisible energy. And the vehicles drive themselves, too. Just get in and say where you need to go. Then sit back, watch a movie, or read a holo-book, and you'll arrive at your destination in a twinkling. It's so easy a kid can do it. In fact they do. Starlings of any age are allowed to drive!

## SWIFT TRAIN

A network of energy-efficient, on-time trains moves commuters around Starland in total-twinkle comfort.

# STELLAR CELEBRATIONS

Starlings love to celebrate, and they take almost any opportunity to do so. Get a good grade on a test? Sparkle party! Make a new friend? Time for a star-lebration!

## LIGHT GIVING DAY

On the first day of the Time of New Beginnings, Starlings exchange glowing gifts with one another. Community picnics and games mark the occasion and celebrate the return of longer, warmer days.

## FESTIVAL OF ILLUMINATION

Arriving midway through the Time of Shadows, this holiday is a
welcome break from the bleak cold season. It's a celebration of lights
and family. Millions of tiny twinkle lights cover buildings and hang in
the sky. Music, dancing, special foods, and sharing the love of family
lift everybody's spirits during this dreary time of year.

# STARSHINE DAY

This sizzling holiday celebrates Starland and the outdoors. It comes during the Time of Lumiere, the warmest part of the year. Outdoor festivals, water sports, and the annual star ball championship tournament make this a holiday everyone enjoys.

## WISH GIVING

The very best wishes are shared among family and friends at this celebration of gratitude. It comes after the harvest, in the Time of Letting Go. It's all about coming together to share in a feast and celebrate the people you care about.

STARLING ACADEMY

## STARLING ACADEMY

Starland's most esteemed boarding school is Starling Academy. Located on the shores of Luminous Lake, the campus is between Starland City and the soaring Crystal Mountains. The dramatic setting has been an inspiration to students for hundreds of years. The brightest young Starlings come here from all parts of Starland to pursue their dreams and do their parts to ensure that Starland will flourish for light-years to come.

# STELLAR SCHOOL

Starling Academy is a respected four-year girls' school, dedicated to wish granting and its associated talents. The entrance exam is super challenging, and getting accepted is quite an honor. The good news for parents is that the cost for such a star-studded education is exactly zero. Cosmic rays!

Students learn energy manipulation, wishful thinking, shooting star travel, and much more. Of course, not everyone who attends wants to be—or will qualify to be—a Wish-Granter. But no matter what their majors, students at Starling Academy can count on getting the universe's most stellar education.

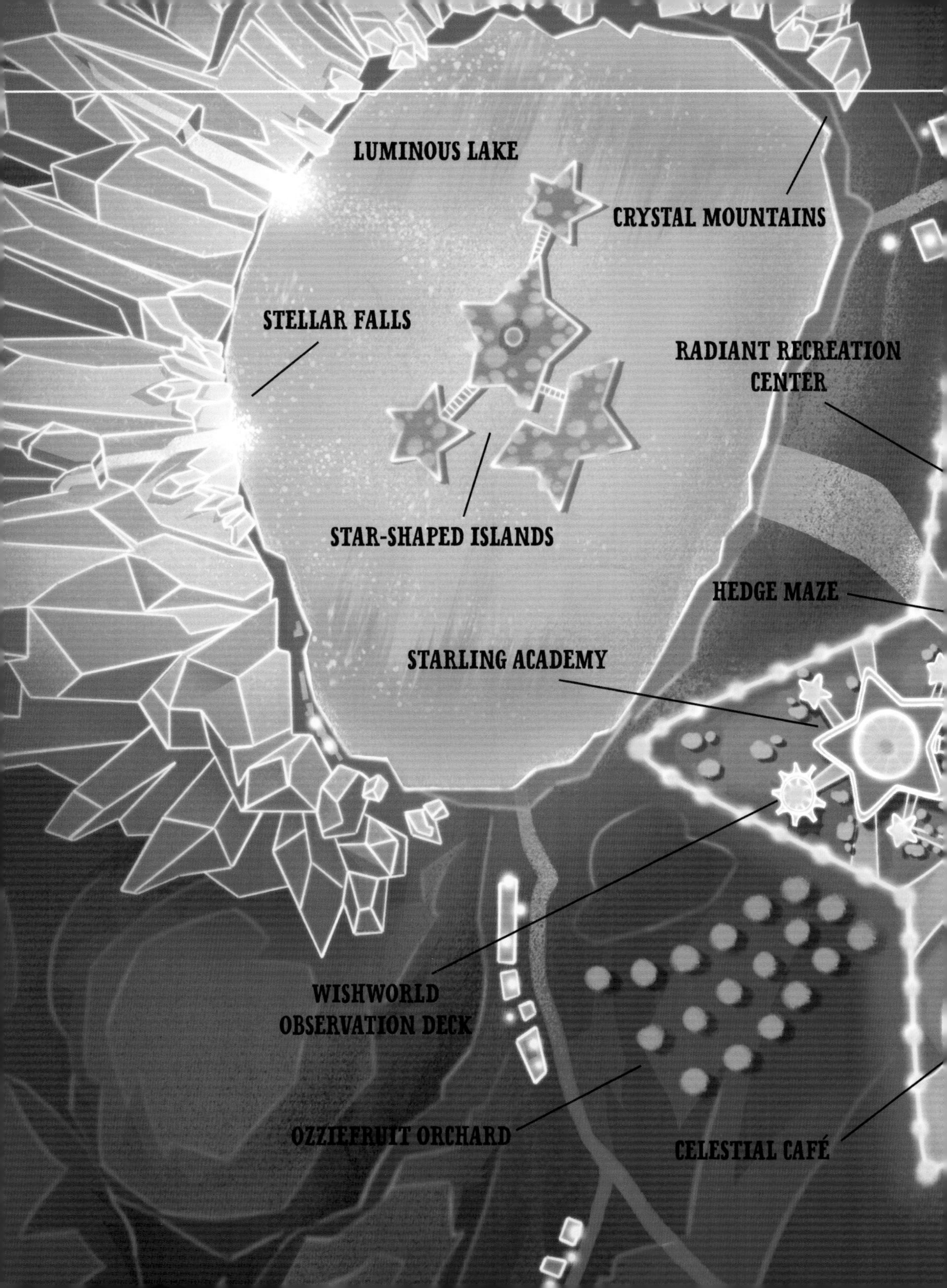

LUMINOUS LAKE

CRYSTAL MOUNTAINS

STELLAR FALLS

RADIANT RECREATION
CENTER

STAR-SHAPED ISLANDS

HEDGE MAZE

STARLING ACADEMY

WISHWORLD
OBSERVATION DECK

OZZIEFRUIT ORCHARD

CELESTIAL CAFÉ

# TOUR THE CAMPUS

TEACHERS' RESIDENCES

ORCHARD

LITTLE DIPPER DORMITORY

BIG DIPPER DORMITORY

CONSTELLATION LANE

GATE TO STARLING ACADEMY

ILLUMINATION LIBRARY

BAND SHELL

ORCHARD

# STAR STUDENT
# DORMS

Starling Academy students are housed in two dormitories. The metallic buildings are built for comfort and fun, with brightly colored twinkly lights.

The Little Dipper Dorm is for first- and second-year students. Even though it's the smaller of the two dorms, it holds more students because the rooms are more compact. The Big Dipper Dorm is for third- and fourth-year students. The older girls enjoy larger rooms and an awesome rooftop deck with lounge chairs for hanging out with friends and stargazing.

All students live two to a pod in adjoining rooms and are allowed to design their personal space however they want. That makes for a lot of individual sparkle and whimsy!

THE STAR DARLINGS WHO
LIVE IN LITTLE DIPPER ARE:

Sage and Cassie, Libby and Gemma
Piper and Vega, Clover and Astra

THE STAR DARLINGS WHO
LIVE IN BIG DIPPER ARE:

Scarlet and Leona, Tessa and Adora

# SAGE'S ROOM

Sage's room had to be all lavender and shades of the same color, and she chose a circular design because she likes the way a circle never ends. Sage also loves plants, so she has one on either side of her bed. Their soft glow provides a natural calming night-light.

Her comfy circular chair is perfect for reading, taking a nap, or just daydreaming. Sage's porthole windows are holo-powered. She designed and programmed them to enhance or redirect her mood. If Sage doesn't like the weather, she can change the view outside the window!

# CASSIE'S ROOM

One look at Cassie's space and you can tell what she loves to do: read! Shelves of holo-books ring Cassie's cozy room. Her bed is placed above it all at the top of a glowing curved stairway.

Cassie programs her holo-wall to wrap her in images of Starland's flora and fauna. It helps her feel connected. But her absolute favorite feature is her curl-up personal reading nook, tucked next to the massive picture window. With its huge assortment of pillows, it's the perfect place to read her mysteries and keep her eyes on the stars.

# LIBBY'S ROOM

Libby loves beautiful things and took a great deal of care designing her room. Her favorite color is everywhere—on the walls, the bed, the rug—just about everything is pink! The room sparkles with a thousand lights. The walls, the star flowers, the bed platform, and even the carpet twinkle.

The space is practical, too. Libby loves having visitors and has a closet full of folding chairs. When she's alone, she practices her keytar in front of her full-length mirror, which is equipped with a holo-recorder so she can record and play back her performances!

# GEMMA'S ROOM

Gemma's room has a super-stellar speaker system in the bed and on the chair so she can play music for her friends when they come to hang. She likes to have people over as much as possible. She could chat with her friends all day—which is why when she isn't with them she can still use her huge computer screen to chat with them, all at once if she wants to. It's equipped to show up to six different full-sized holo-chat windows! If anyone can keep six convos going at once, it's Gemma!

When she can't find anyone to gab with, she's got a skylight for stargazing and a reclining chair for dreaming and looking out the window.

# PIPER'S ROOM

Piper has the most private space of all the Star Darlings. The top floor is a circular design that removes her from the rest of the world. Soothing fragrances given off by carefully selected plants perfume the air. Piper can spend hours there reflecting on the things that matter to her most.

Her jewel-toned padded bed is in the center. Its circular sides are lined with twinkling lights. Except for a few floor pillows, the bed is Piper's only piece of furniture. If she wants to be with friends, she goes down a steep spiral stairway to the lower level. Scarlet likes to visit just so she can ride her skateboard down!

# VEGA'S ROOM

Vega's room is lush and plush and boasts a spot for everything that's important to her. She's divided the space with thick area rugs in midnight blue flecked with twinkling mini stars.

The bed has an overhanging headboard that adds a touch of both comfort and coziness. It's the perfect spot for reading, thinking, and getting the best sleep possible. Steps lead to a stage that allows her to rock out by herself or with the band. But the ceiling is the room's most striking feature. It has a huge glass skylight that allows for hours of stargazing. It's her portal to the worlds beyond.

# CLOVER'S ROOM

Clover's space is practical, interesting, and fun. She wanted an extra-high ceiling so she could practice her juggling, and she misses her family so she keeps in touch through several state-of-the-art monitors. Because music is Clover's life, she has an area dedicated to recording new songs and practicing her DJ skills. The huge plush couch is so comfy there are times when friends just don't want to leave!

Clover's time with the circus really shows in her choice of sleeping spaces. She prefers a hammock instead of a regular bed. But it's the floor of her room that has the most awesome feature—an underground terrarium!

# ASTRA'S ROOM

Astra's room is perfect for an athlete, especially a brilliant star ball player. With a built-in court and holo-net, she can practice shooting anytime she wishes. Even cooler than that, the main wall in her room allows her to feel like she's inside a full-sized star ball court, or even a star bases stadium! There's a special area to store and display all her athletic equipment and her many impressive holo-trophies. And when she needs to relax after a game, she's got a sunken circular couch where she can stretch out and recharge.

# SCARLET'S ROOM

Scarlet designed her space so she can skateboard down its walls. Good thing her board doesn't leave scuff marks! Her drum set is up on a small platform. But no worries about the noise problem; if Leona needs to study, Scarlet can flick on the drum system's self-muting switch and play silent beats all day and night.

Scarlet's staircase leads to a small nook, where she can go for some frequently needed alone time.

# LEONA'S ROOM

Leona's space is dazzling. The gold colors twinkle and shine almost as much as Leona does! The bed's starlight curtain and ball light keep her bathed in brightness.

She has her own stage, too—a mini star-shaped platform that rises up from the floor when she wants to rehearse or perform for her friends. Leona's holo-wall includes a premium sound system and different holographic audience settings. She can switch among a small café audience, students cheering at the band shell, and a megawatt stadium crowd!

# TESSA'S ROOM

Tessa's space is a brilliantly comfy place where she can go to refuel. Literally. She has a table that's always covered with samples of the delicious treats she loves. Her bed is ultra plush, she has a chair covered with cozy fabric that conforms to the shape of her body when she snuggles into it, and her rug is celestially soft.

Tessa's holo-wall displays the fruits and vegetables that are in season to inspire her recipes. And her headboard features a screen with virtual pets she can care for now that she doesn't get to interact with the animals on her family's farm every day.

mountainous skyline right outside her windows. Inside the cozy space, she has everything a budding science fashionista needs. Adora's got the lab equipment to develop and create a new type of fabric or an extra-shimmery sequin, plus space to neatly store her bolts of fabric and a star-sewing machine that can stitch fabric at light speed.

Her bed is round and very soft, and the giant headboard is a holo-display of her scientific equations; so when Adora's not sleeping, she can always see what she's working on, in case the perfect fashion solution suddenly comes to her in a flash of genius!

# TYPICAL SCHEDULES

### SAGE'S CLASSES:

**First-Year Student**
1. Wishers 101
2. Intro to Wish Identification
3. Wishful Thinking
4. Astral Accounting
5. Lighterature
6. Intro to Wish Fulfillment
7. The Golden Days
8. P.E. (Physical Energy)
9. Aspirational Art

### ASTRA'S CLASSES:

**Second-Year Student**
1. Wishful Thinking
2. Wish Theory
3. Astral Accounting
4. Chronicle Class
5. Color Catching
6. Practice Wish Orb Lab II
7. Aspirational Art
8. Light Casting
9. Advanced P.E.

### TESSA'S CLASSES:

**Third-Year Student**
1. Advanced Wish Theory
2. Wishworld Relations
3. Wish Fulfillment
4. Wish Energy Capture
5. Wish Wrangling
6. Advanced Astral Accounting
7. Wish Orb Tending
8. Practice Wish Orb Mastery
9. Intuition
10. Music Jam

# CLASS SCHEDULES

Starling Academy keeps students moving at light speed with a super-full constellation of classes. They're expected to sign up for between eight and ten classes each semester. Of course the focus is on wish granting, but there are plenty of other subjects that students can pursue.

Classrooms are located in the Starling Academy building and in a few other places around campus. Holo-walls, holo-books, and superstar computers are standard in every classroom. The bigger rooms are for the classes everyone has to take, such as Wishers 101 and The Golden Days, a class about Starland's history. The smaller classrooms are for more advanced classes and seminars.

# HALO HALL

Halo Hall is Starling Academy's most famous building. It's known throughout Starland as the shining symbol of the academy. The enormous star-shaped structure seems to float above the ground on a fountain of streaming wish energy. The building's glistening surface reflects the stars, campus lights, and flickering energy around it in an ever-changing light show. A star beacon shoots out of the center of the structure's domed hub, symbolizing the power of wish energy.

The building contains offices for the academy's staff and faculty, as well as classrooms and the Astral Auditorium. The auditorium is the first stop for new students; it's where Lady Stella welcomes every incoming freshman class and introduces them to campus life. The interactive auditorium, which uses technology that stimulates the five senses, is also where general assemblies, shows, and graduation ceremonies take place.

Right behind the building is another famous structure. It's an almost impossibly tall tower with the Wishworld Observation Deck at the top. That's where school officials go to keep tabs on missions to Wishworld.

# STAR QUAD

Star Quad is in the center of everything and anchors the campus. Arranged around it are the dorms, the library, the café, Halo Hall, and the recreation center.

There's a star fountain in the middle of the plaza, along with benches and comfortable spots to have a snack or a picnic lunch. The band shell, between the Celestial Café and the fountain, hosts everything from talent shows to full-scale concerts. On the other side of the fountain is a startastic hedge maze. Some students like to race through it, competing for the best time. Others just lazily stroll through. One supercool thing is that the maze changes from time to time, sometimes while students are in it!

# BAND SHELL

The band shell is the outdoor performance space for the academy's music program. Soloists, orchestras, and rock bands all play there.

The band shell is like no other. It looks normal enough, but it has the unique ability to change its shape according to what's being played onstage. For a small string quartet, the walls of the enclosure move in to focus the sound. For a rock band, the band shell flares out as wide as it can. Starmazing, right?

Below the band shell is the home of the music program. There are classrooms, rehearsal rooms, listening rooms, a recording studio, and tons of instruments.

# ILLUMINATION LIBRARY

The Illumination Library is impressively huge and holds just about every holo-book ever written. There are also special collections on very specific topics—such as the origins of negative energy—and a catalog of every cool gadget invented on Starland.

Holo-books are similar to books on Wishworld but aren't printed. They're stored in holo-holders that flip open and project the pages into the air. The holders can store thousands of books.

Like any library, the Illumination Library is a quiet place designed for research, study, and reflection. The staff is well trained and super helpful. Just outside the main library is the Lightning Lounge. Students love to hang out there. For one thing, it's packed with free snacks. The lounge has comfortable couches and chairs, soft rugs, and overstuffed pillows. Two fireplaces sit at either end of the room, and the roof retracts so students can watch the stars.

# CELESTIAL CAFÉ

The Celestial Café is not what you would call your typical school cafeteria. Unlike the ones on Wishworld, this cafeteria has almost anything you could want to eat, everything is totally fresh, and, most important, it all tastes startastic!

A typical meal might start with a salad of lighttuce and featherjaffer with light vinaigrette. After that, perhaps some roasted druderwomp medallions with a side of garble greens. For dessert, frozen glorange crystals served with a cup of hot Zing is popular. Super stellar!

Students sit at large round tables to encourage socializing. Judging by the noise level in the dining room, there's no shortage of that. Bot-Bot waiters buzz around, bringing any foods the girls request and cleaning up the dishes. Watching them try to avoid running into the students is a favorite pastime.

# RADIANT RECREATION CENTER

The Radiant Recreation Center is where students take Physical Energy (P.E.), health, and fitness classes. There's a large gymnasium for exercising, a running track, gaming areas, and a sparkling star-pool. Outside is a playing field with bleachers on both sides.

Though the main focus of the academy is squarely on wish fulfillment, students are encouraged to get involved in sports. In fact, the school is super proud of its star ball team. The game is kind of like basketball on Wishworld, but players use their energy manipulation skills to move the ball down the court.

Starling Academy's team is called the Glowin' Glions. Over the years, they've won lots of championships. Their mascot, Glarry the Glion, can be seen on mugs, T-shirts, and backpacks all over campus. Astra is the Glowin' Glions' star player!

# THE CRYSTAL MOUNTAINS AND UNDERGROUND CAVERN

The sparkling Crystal Mountains are one of the most celebrated natural wonders on Starland. Starlings come from all over to hike glasslike trails, explore crystalline caves, and admire the brilliant Stellar Falls.

Luminous Lake lies at the foot of the mountains, with the Starling Academy campus set on the other side. The lake's lustrous surface glows and shimmers with every shade of blue. Several small islands, linked by footbridges, are set in the middle of the lake. Accessible only by boat, the islands are the home of the inspirational Serenity Gardens, Starland's showcase for its fabulous flora. The gardens overflow with lush flowering trees and shrubs, hanging gardens, tangled multicolored vines, and stone pathways.

Deep beneath Starling Academy is a long-forgotten underground cavern that serves as the Star Darlings' secret headquarters. It's where Lady Stella can train the girls without worrying about other faculty or students walking in. It's also where the Wish Pendants and Power Crystals are stored for safekeeping.

FACULTY AND STUDENTS

## FACULTY AND STUDENTS

With 1,800 students, Starling Academy has pretty much every personality type you can imagine. But the students all have one thing in common: they're brilliant and super motivated to succeed.

As Starland's most prestigious educational facility, it's only natural that Starling Academy would attract the very best instructors to its campus.

When they're not busy illuminating the brightest minds on Starland, faculty members relax in their on-campus homes, situated behind the Radiant Recreation Center. The area is referred to by students as StarProf Row. Each home has a small yard, a garden, and a fantastic view of the Crystal Mountains.

# LADY STELLA

Lady Stella, the headmistress of Starling Academy, radiates wisdom and authority. She's respected on campus and throughout all of Starland as a powerful Wish-Granter. Stella is a fair and kind-hearted woman but can be stern when the situation requires it. She's also well known for her creative problem solving.

Lady Stella is always looking for a solution, which is why she recruited the Star Darlings entirely in secret after coming across the ancient oracle in a long-forgotten book. She believes the twelve girls can fulfill the prophecy by sneaking off to Wishworld and granting the wishes of young Wishlings. Though this has never been tried before, Lady Stella is just bold enough to attempt it.

# LADY CORDIAL

When Lady Cordial was hired as the head of admissions, many wondered what Lady Stella saw in her. The new staff member wasn't at all interested in making friends with the rest of the faculty. There just seemed to be something off-kilter about her.

But as time went on, Lady Cordial proved to be a star at her job. The admissions office was running more efficiently than ever and parent complaints were way down. After that, the faculty and staff put their concerns aside and just tried to stay out of her way.

# PROFESSOR FINDLEY CLAXWORTH

As a professor of Aspirational Art, Claxworth believes in helping every student get in touch with her inner weirdness. And he makes himself a kooky shining example: Professor Claxworth is known for wearing the same paint-splattered smock every day and dancing around campus to a tune nobody else can hear! But for all his quirks, he's fair, even-tempered, and liked by almost everyone.

Art on Starland is typically created through manipulating objects and materials with wish energy, and Claxworth's a master. His abstract paintings hang in several of Starland's finest museums.

# PROFESSOR EUGENIA BRIGHT

Professor Bright came to Starling Academy at the zenith of her career as a master Wish-Granter because she had a strong desire to teach young people what she had learned. She quickly earned the respect of the faculty, and her rapport with students made her everyone's favorite teacher. Her Wish Fulfillment class has a permanent waiting list.

Wish-Granters deal with emotions and the precious dreams of Wishlings. The professor encourages the girls to talk about their own hopes and dreams. Bright believes it's that kind of sensitivity that separates a good Wish-Granter from a great one.

# PROFESSOR DOLORES RAYE

Professor Raye is a nuts-and-bolts, by-the-book instructor. She can be short and impatient with students and has a reputation for being the exact opposite of Professor Bright. She teaches about the manipulation of wish energy, and students who take one of her Wishful Thinking classes quickly learn she is all business. Wish energy is not something to be trifled with, as Professor Raye points out constantly. But because of her dedication, when her students graduate and go to Wishworld, they really know what they're doing.

# PROFESSOR NICOLA CECELIA

Most students assume that anyone who teaches Astral Accounting will be a tough teacher. But Professor Cecelia truly wants all her students to do well. She works overtime to find creative ways to make the topic understandable and—*gasp*—even fun!

Now, that doesn't mean her class is easy. Professor Cecelia expects the most of her clever young students, because they are the best and she knows they can do the most difficult math problems! She challenges her girls to find equations in the stars and believes in their potential!

# PROFESSOR MARGARET DUMARRE

As a leading Wishworld ambassador, Professor Dumarre has studied Wishlings for many years. So it made perfect sense for her to teach classes in the ways of Wishlings. Professor Dumarre is a fantastic listener (that's how she learned so much about Wishlings). She also finds Wishlings humorous, maybe because of her own odd sense of humor. It's almost like all her time on Wishworld has made her more ... human, more casual and grounded. Plus, she can do spot-on imitations of Wishlings that delight the girls. Her class, Wishworld Relations, is fun, and students get the lowdown on what Wishworld is really like from someone who's been there.

# PROFESSOR RUPERT DAG

Rupert Dag teaches Astronomics. Buttoned-up and by the numbers, Professor Dag is kind of a sourpuss but greatly respected. Astronomics is a dry profession—basically math and accounting as applied to space and energy principles—so the people involved in it tend to be starched, stiff, awkward, and nerdy. But they are also incredibly brilliant, and no one can deny that Professor Dag is all those things!

# PROFESSOR ELARA URSA

Professor Ursa teaches Wishers 101. As one of the best Wish-Granters in Starling history, she has been to Wishworld almost as much as Professor Dumarre. But while Dumarre loves Wishlings, Ursa has become completely disenchanted with them. She thinks Wishlings are gross and loud and wasteful; so even though she's supposed to be informing her students about Wishlings, she ends up really freaking them out!

# PROFESSOR LUCRETIA DELPHINUS

Professor Delphinus teaches Wish Identification class. She helps the girls figure out how to tell what kind of wish is which and how to find the Wisher when they get to Wishworld. She is very tiny but tough, and she likes to sit on the edge of a table when she lectures so she doesn't seem so small. The problem is she sometimes has to try jumping two or three times to make it up onto the table!

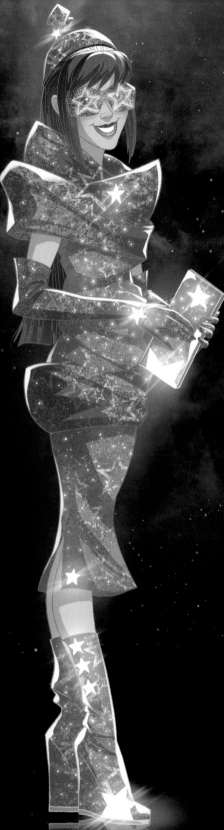

# PROFESSOR ILLUMIA WICKES

Professor Wickes teaches Wish Theory. She is airy, brainy, and eccentric, and her method of teaching is to let her students talk while she guides the conversation. Wish Theory is like philosophy in that it is all about ideas. The people who are into it are usually the same ones who like debating concepts and viewpoints, and they tend to have quick minds and sharp tongues. Her class is a favorite with the chattier, more vocal students.

# VIVICA

Vivica longs to be the center of attention. When she saw that twelve girls had the same message on their Star-Zaps that used the acronym SD and said to report to Lady Stella's office, she was instantly jealous. So she said it stood for Star Dipper, to mock the girls. And, of course, since the Star Darlings' cover story is that they're part of a remedial class, the label stuck.

Vivica is only in her first year, but she's determined to be the most popular girl in school. And if that means taking down the twelve SDs, then that's just what she'll do!

# BOT-BOT MO-J4

Bot-Bot guides roam the campus to direct students to classes and just be generally helpful. But MO-J4 isn't an ordinary robot. When he led Sage on her campus tour, something sparked inside him. Quite unexpectedly, he formed an attachment to Sage and wanted to help her however he could. Sage is star-stoked about that. He makes her laugh and has a heart of gold!

# CLASSMATES AND DUDES

The other students at Starling Academy come from all kinds of backgrounds and have a variety of interests, but each one is a high achiever. Slackers need not apply!

There are no male Starlings at the academy, but across Luminous Lake is a similar all-boys school, called Star Prep. Though the two academies occasionally have events together, like the Shining Star Dance, they usually do their own thing.

# WISHWORLD

## WISHWORLD

To Starlings, the most amazing thing about Earth is the vast number of wishes made every day. So it only makes sense that they call it Wishworld.

# WHAT WISHLINGS WISH UPON

Wishlings seem to have an endless number of things that inspire them to wish. Some are common all across Wishworld, and some are known only in a particular region. But no matter what the Wishling uses to make a wish, what's important is the purity of the wish itself.

A GOOD WISH is one that asks for positive things, such as becoming more confident, helping a friend, or pursuing a dream.

A BAD WISH is one made for selfish reasons or with the intent to harm someone. Granting a bad wish releases destructive negative energy, which Starlings try to avoid at all costs.

An IMPOSSIBLE WISH asks for something that Starlings are simply not able to grant, such as for the world to be made of chocolate or for the Wishling to live forever.

# WISH UPON . . .

**A STAR** When you see a shooting star or the first star of the evening, hold your wish in your imagination and say:

*Star light, star bright, the first star I see tonight:*
*I wish I may, I wish I might, have the wish I wish tonight.*

**BIRTHDAY CANDLES** Make a wish, then blow out all your birthday candles in one breath.

**A DANDELION** Pick a dandelion full of fluffy seeds. With the wind to your back, close your eyes, make a wish, and blow as hard as you can.

**A COIN** Stand with your back to a fountain or a wishing well. Throw a coin over your shoulder and make a wish.

**A WISHBONE** Let a wishbone dry out until it is brittle. Then hold one end of the wishbone and have a friend hold the other end. Make a wish and pull. Whoever gets the larger piece will have his or her wish come true.

**A RAINBOW** The moment you see a rainbow, make a wish.

## OTHER WAYS THAT WISHLINGS WISH:

- ✦ Catch a falling leaf. Hold it tight and make a wish.
- ✦ Find a four-leaf clover. Make a wish and let it go.
- ✦ When you see the first full moon of the year, make a wish.
- ✦ If you lose an eyelash, put it on your fingertip. Close your eyes, make a wish, and blow the eyelash away.

# CATCH A RIDE ON A SHOOTING STAR

The galaxy is full of shooting stars. And that's a good thing for Starlings. Not only are shooting stars lovely to see, but they're practical, too. Starlings ride them to Wishworld! A Starling uses a powerful ball of wish energy to attach herself to the passing star. Once she arrives on Wishworld, she detaches herself and uses energy manipulation to land softly on the ground. The trip is like the most amazing thrill ride ever! Then, the shooting star shrinks down to a magical mini-star that the Starling can fold up and keep in her pocket.

When the mission is over, the Wish-Granter uses the burst of positive wish energy that comes from a granted wish to whoosh herself back to Starland. But if her mission isn't successful, she can always reactivate her magical mini-star to get home.

So the next time you see a shooting star, you'll know that someone's wish is about to come true. Maybe even yours!

# WISH MISSIONS

The first wishes ever granted were fulfilled by Starlings who never left Starland! Starlings learned that once a Wish Orb began to sparkle they could actually go *into* it. Inside was the world of the Wisher, like an interactive holo-dome. From there, the Starling could use her talents to grant the wish long-distance.

Over time, Starlings figured out that they could collect far more positive wish energy by granting the wish in person instead of using the orb. It's done that way practically all the time now, but the orbs are still used occasionally.

Students at Starling Academy use Practice Wish Orbs—devices made to function like real Wish Orbs—to learn how to grant wishes. Only those who earn a degree in wish granting will be able to go on to do "in-person" Wish Missions after graduation (with the exception of the twelve Star Darlings, of course).

On Wishworld, Starlings have to blend in to be effective. The cloaking function on their Wish Pendants has the power to totally change their appearance—right down to the clothes they wear.

# WISH PENDANTS

Wish Pendants are given to Wish-Granters before their first Wish Mission. The magical devices are the key to every mission's success. On Starland, the pendant absorbs wish energy that can be used on Wishworld to help grant a wish. The pendant contains a cloaking device to disguise the Starling—one touch and the pendant masks her glow, takes the sparkle from her skin, and changes her hair color and clothing. Pendants also have a Wisher locator. Once the wish is granted, the Wish Pendant absorbs the positive wish energy and carries it back to Starland.

Even though the Star Darlings haven't graduated to full-fledged Wish-Granters yet, Lady Stella has equipped each girl with her own Wish Pendant. Super celestial!

### STAR PENDANT
Sage's gold star glows brightly when the pendant takes on wish energy.

### STAR BOOT BUCKLES
Scarlet's buckles light up one at a time as she closes in on her Wisher.

## GOLD STAR BRACELET

The outer ring of Leona's bracelet glimmers as she gets nearer to her Wisher.

## STAR NECKLACE

Light flickers across Libby's constellation of stars when it detects positive wish energy.

## STAR BELT BUCKLE

The points on Vega's belt buckle direct her to her Wisher.

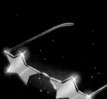

## GOLD STAR BANGLES

The stars on Piper's bracelets flicker in sequence when the Wisher is near.

## STAR WRISTBANDS

Astra's single-star bands work together to guide her to her target. If the left star lights, turn left; right, turn right.

## STAR GLASSES

Pulses of light chase around the rims of Cassie's glasses when she's getting close to her Wisher.

## STAR BARRETTE

Clover's barrette glows when she's close to her Wisher.

## STAR BROOCH

The tips of the star on Tessa's brooch light up to point the way to the one she's supposed to help.

## STAR EARRINGS

Gemma's bold earrings light up, but they also beep softly when her Wisher is nearby.

## STAR WATCH

Adora's watch emits a blue glow as soon as it detects a Wisher's energy.

# GLOSSARY

**BAD WISH ORBS:** Orbs that are from cruel or selfish wishes. They are quickly sent to the Negative Energy Facility.

**BAND SHELL:** A covered stage located in the Star Quad.

**BRIGHT DAY:** The day a Starling is born.

**CELESTIAL CAFÉ:** Starling Academy's outstanding cafeteria.

**CRYSTAL MOUNTAINS:** The most beautiful mountains on Starland; located across the lake from Starling Academy.

**FESTIVAL OF ILLUMINATION:** A celebration of lights and family that comes midway through the Time of Shadows.

**GLAMERA:** A holographic image recording device.

**GLOWIN' GLIONS:** Starling Academy's top-ranked star ball team.

**ILLUMINATION LIBRARY:** The impressive library at Starling Academy.

**IMPOSSIBLE WISHES:** Wishes that are beyond the power of Starlings to grant.

**KEYTAR:** Like a guitar but with keys instead of strings.

**LIGHT GIVING DAY:** A holiday held on the first day of the Time of New Beginnings. It celebrates renewal and the return of warmer weather.

**LUMINOUS LAKE:** A serene and lovely lake next to the Starling Academy campus.

**POWER CRYSTAL:** The powerful stone that each Star Darling receives once she has granted her first wish.

**RADIANT RECREATION CENTER:** Starling Academy's fitness and sports center.

**SERENITY GARDENS:** Extensive botanical gardens set on an island in Luminous Lake.

**SHOOTING STARS:** Speeding stars that Starlings can latch on to and ride to Wishworld.

**SILVER BLOSSOM:** The final manifestation of a Good Wish Orb, this glimmering metallic bloom is placed in the Hall of Granted Wishes.

**SPARKLE SHOWER:** An energy shower Starlings take every day to get clean and refresh their sparkling glow.

**STAR BALL:** An intramural sport that shares similarities with basketball on Wishworld. But star ball players use energy manipulation to control the ball.

**STARCAR:** The primary mode of transportation for most Starlings. These ultra-safe vehicles drive themselves on a cushion of wish energy.

**STAR DARLINGS:** The twelve Star-Charmed Starlings chosen by Lady Stella to go on top-secret missions to Wishworld.

**STARLAND:** An irregularly shaped world veiled by a bright yellow glow that, from a distance, makes it look like a regular star.

**STARLAND CITY:** The largest city on Starland is also its capital.

**STARLING ACADEMY:** The most prestigious all-girl four-year boarding school for wish granting on Starland.

**STARLINGS:** The glowing beings with sparkly skin that live on Starland.

**STAR QUAD:** The central part of the Starling Academy campus.

**STARSHINE DAY:** A holiday held in the middle of the hottest time of year, the Time of Lumiere.

**STAR-ZAP:** A handheld device that Starlings use for almost everything.

**TIME OF LETTING GO:** One of the four seasons on Starland. It falls between the warmest season and the coldest.

**TIME OF LUMIERE:** The warmest season on Starland.

**TIME OF NEW BEGINNINGS:** The season that follows the coldest time of year; it's when plants and trees come into bloom.

**TIME OF SHADOWS:** The coldest season of the year on Starland.

**TOOTHLIGHT:** A high-tech gadget that Starlings use to clean their teeth.

**WISH BLOSSOM:** The bloom that appears from a Wish Orb after its wish is granted.

**WISH ENERGY:** The positive energy that is released when a wish is granted. Wish energy powers everything on Starland.

**WISH GIVING:** A celebration of gratitude for friends and family that is held after the harvest in the Time of Letting Go.

**WISH-HOUSE:** The place where Wish Orbs are cared for until they sparkle. Once the orb's wish is granted, it becomes a Wish Blossom.

**WISH MISSION:** The task Starlings undertake when they travel to Wishworld to help grant a wish.

**WISH ORB:** The form a wish takes on Wishworld before traveling to Starland. There it will grow and sparkle when it's time to grant the wish.

**WISH PENDANT:** A gadget that absorbs and transports wish energy, helps Starlings locate their Wishers, and contains a cloaking device.

**WISHWORLD:** The planet that Starland relies on for wish energy. The beings on Wishworld know it by another name—Earth.